I0728035

Cowboys and Aliens: An Alien Scifi Romance

DEMELZA CARLTON

ONE

"All right, everyone, you know the drill. On three. One, two, three…Haaaappy birthday…" Rana's voice was quickly drowned out by the rest of the office as they took up the song. She'd never admit it to anyone, but this was why she organised birthday morning teas for the office. Not for the cake, not for the smiles, though both were wonderful, but for the shared song, air vibrating in a dozen or more throats in harmony and joy. For an air elemental like her, it was as close as she came to bliss these days.

If that cake tasted as good as it looked, this would definitely qualify as her best birthday ever.

"Now cut the cake and make a wish!" someone said.

Rana took the knife gingerly – it was big enough to cut the whole cake in two, and the pastrychef at Sweet Teeth had gone to so much trouble with the airy whirls of cream and frosting – and touched the blade to the top of the cake.

"Make a wish! Make a wish!" It seemed everyone took up the chant.

The blade slid through the cake like it

was little more than air.

She wished…she could make a connection with someone. Someone she could spend time with. It didn't have to be another air elemental – stars knew most of her people had perished when their colony ship, the *Titanic*, had been destroyed at the beginning of the war, blown out with the ship's air supply, to die slowly for want of air and energy in the vacuum of space. No, just someone whose company she enjoyed, who liked spending time with her. Someone who cared enough about her to remember her birthday, and maybe share her birthday dinner tonight, instead of heading home alone to fall into bed, exhausted.

Not that she had time to meet anyone, let alone go out for dinner, lately.

Especially when her boss kept her so busy she could barely catch her breath most days.

"Rana!"

Stars. Was Ira's meeting with Paris over already? Usually his meetings with the counselling staff took longer. The mental health problems in the Colony weren't going to simply go away, not after they'd lost so much, both in leaving their homes and then during the war here.

That's why it was so important to celebrate what they could — birthdays, anniversaries, all the small victories that proclaimed to the universe that they were still here, still fighting to live and be happy.

Rana handed the cake knife to one of

the detectives, excused herself, and headed over to Ira.

"Yes, sir?" she asked, summoning a smile to her face.

He waved his hand. "Is all this really necessary?"

Paris's usually serene countenance darkened with a frown.

Rana's heart went out to her, as she sucked all her courage into her core to strengthen her. He might be a powerful Titan, but she wasn't afraid of him. "Yes, sir, it most certainly is. It's a celebration of another year of life, which none of us were certain of before the peace talks. Every victory should be celebrated, no matter how small. It's also a gesture of appreciation, of thanks for their hard work, because even in the relative peace here in the Colony, it hasn't been easy. Especially with a mixed race force, when Humans were at war with Titans only a short time ago, and now we're working together, sharing a meal together, celebrating together. We're building camaraderie and family, for people who need to know who has their back when they're out there on patrol. The catering is sourced from local businesses, which we're helping support, using food produced right here in the Colony, building goodwill for the Watch in the community. So yes, this is as essential as food or air or water."

At least Paris was smiling again, though Ira's frown had deepened.

"I have clients to see, so I'd best get back to my consulting rooms. Until next month, Ira, if I don't see you earlier," Paris said with a wave as she made her way out of the office.

"So you believe we need a meal to truly bring us together?" Ira asked.

Rana knew that tone. He was looking for an argument, so he could vent about his frustrations, and he expected her to sit and listen, nodding occasionally, until he was done. Well, not today. Today was her birthday, her first ever birthday with a cake and candles, and not even Ira could take that away from her.

"Yes, I do. I mean, during the war and when we were travelling, we all ate together in mess halls. Here in the Colony, we have privacy again, with our own homes, but there's also the danger of loneliness. I mean, sitting alone in your apartment with a ration bar, thinking about everything you've lost, is one of the reasons Paris and the other counsellors have been so busy. That's why there was such a rush to get restaurants open, and agriculture, so we could eat real food again and it means so much more than just choking down a ration bar to sustain yourself for another day. It's about aromas and flavours and textures and conversation and company and togetherness. It's a celebration of who we are, and what we don't want to lose."

Ira blew out a breath, visibly deflating. "Good. Then I need you to plan exactly that kind of celebration for the one year anniversary of the Colony. Paris says we need to celebrate it, and I have no idea where to start. You're perfect. Prepare a contract for yourself as the event coordinator with double your salary from now until the day of the anniversary. No, until the week after it, so you can take that week off. Use whatever resources necessary, within reason. And give me a complete outline of your plans for the event by the end of the week." Ira turned on his heel and headed into his office, shutting the door before Rana could even open her mouth.

Plan a Colony-wide event for thousands of people within a week…why, the anniversary was less than a month away! She wouldn't even know where to start.

"Hey, it's your birthday — don't forget to have some cake!" Detective Minali said, shoving a plate into Rana's hands.

Rana began to spoon cake into her mouth, barely tasting it.

Why couldn't she have kept her mouth shut and just listened to her boss rant? Now she had even more work to do.

Rana dropped the half-eaten cake into the bin, her appetite gone.

This had to be the worst birthday ever.

TWO

No matter how bad the news was, it couldn't be worse than his worst day, Byron told himself. Nothing could be as bad as finding his parents after they'd both taken their own lives, with the blood-splattered farm foreclosure notice on the table between them. Too many years of drought had destroyed them, until they'd seen death as the only way out. Leaving him with no one and nothing.

No matter how bad it was, he still had his new farm in the Colony. It wasn't like he had anyone else left to lose.

So he'd just have to build up the herd with however many cows he had left, and hope they'd eradicated the disease. He'd been so careful, and now he'd be doubly careful, just in case.

Byron glanced at his tablet again. Yes, the message was still there. He was to meet with the bioengineer at the door to Farm 3, Lower Level of the Arena Dome, in less than an hour, to discuss lifting the quarantine. If everything went well, as he knew it must, he'd be feeding the cows before day's end. Stars knew he'd had enough bad luck already — surely the universe couldn't give him any more.

The aircar was empty except for him. No events in the Arena Stadium today, then, he guessed, or the aircar and the platform would be packed with people. He vaguely recalled seeing some advertising for a battle between some men and a dragon to take place in the Stadium when he'd been stuck in that box of a temporary apartment while his own ranch house was under quarantine, but he hadn't been paying attention. It wasn't like he intended to watch some poor creature get slaughtered for sport. No, farmers tended to take death seriously. Sure, they slaughtered their animals for meat, or sent them off to market, knowing that was their fate, but that was for food. Survival. Making sure people's most basic needs were met. And, while they were in his care, ensuring the health and welfare of his stock.

Which was why he was already in the Arena Dome, almost an hour early. He wanted to see his herd. The station platform was just as empty as the aircar as Byron headed for the ramp to the lower levels. He expected the tunnels to be empty, as they usually were, for there were only farms and farmers' apartments down there, but crates were stacked along the wall, all the way from the bottom of the ramp to the door to Farm

3. The doorway itself was blocked by several people, all wearing the telltale green coveralls that marked them as bioengineers. Byron had rarely seen so many of them in one place, outside of the Eden Dome where the bioengineering labs were.

One figure, slightly shorter than the rest, made a dismissive gesture and the others headed in his direction. When they reached him, they didn't stop – they merely paused to exchange nods of acknowledgement before they were on their way. Back to Eden, most likely, where, rumour had it, they all had apartments overlooking the nature biomes. The best views in the Colony, or so he'd been told.

The small, green-clad figure turned to face him. "You're early, Mr Kidd."

Byron shrugged. "Can you blame me? I don't like living in a box. I'm eager to go home."

She scrunched up her nose. "Well, you'll be happy to know, my staff have done a complete decontamination of the entire farm, right down to the soil. There's no trace of the disease left."

"Were you able to identify it?" The last thing Byron wanted was for some new, alien disease to be killing his cattle. He'd had enough fighting aliens in the war against the Titans.

"Yes. It's a transmissible spongiform encephalopathy which matches those found on Earth. We tested all the animals in your herd, as well as the embryos still in the lab. They all tested positive, I'm afraid, and we had to destroy them," she said.

Byron blinked. "I'm sorry... you... what?"

"We destroyed them, Mr Kidd. It looks like that entire crop of embryos was infected, long before they left Earth. We suspect some mistake must have been made by the Earth labs where the embryos came from. Instead of sending healthy embryos, suitable for colony breeding stock, they sent us embryos destined for a lab that was studying the disease, likely taken from euthanised infected pregnant cows. So far, we've only tested one batch, which was used to produce all your stock, and it remains to be seen whether the other embryo batches are also infected. If they are, we'll have to look at other livestock for Farm 3. We have sheep, kangaroos, emus and camels…do you have a preference?"

Kangaroos and camels? Was she serious? Byron tried to keep his voice even. "Look, lady…whatever your name is…"

"Lilith," she supplied. "Doctor Lilith Zielinski."

Of course she was some sort of doctor. All the bioengineers had PhDs. "Okay, Doctor Lilith," he began again. "I signed up for the Colony because I have experience running a remote cattle station. That means cows. I wouldn't know anything about farming those other things. I definitely don't know anything about a transmissible sponge…whatever it is. But I am good with cows."

"And bananas, apparently," she said, pointing at the crates. "The guy who dropped those off insisted only you could ripen them properly, so he left them here for you to take care of."

Byron held up his hands. "Okay, I'm good with cows and bananas. But not much else. So, for a poor farmer who doesn't have your academic education…give it to me straight, Doc. How many cows are left in my herd?"

She frowned. "I just told you, we had to destroy them all. Zoonoses like these are highly contagious within the host species, as well as being transmissible to Humans. We couldn't take any chances."

No cows. They'd taken the whole herd and left him with nothing. It was enough to drive a grown man to tears. In fact, Byron felt his left eye prickling. Almost as if…

"No." Byron hadn't meant to say the word aloud, but he didn't want to look like a crazy idiot in front of the bioengineer, so he continued, "No, we can't take any chances. I wouldn't want to lose any more of them to that horrible disease. When…when will you know if the other embryos are safe to develop?"

Lilith shrugged. "When my staff are done testing them. Could be a week, could be six. I don't know. We'll let you know when we do. In the meantime, I can tell you it's safe for you to move back in, and for those bananas." She stared hungrily at the crates. "Is there any chance you could send word when they're ready to go to market? I can't remember the last time I had fresh bananas."

Byron wanted to tell her where she could shove a banana, but he didn't. The disease wasn't her fault – she'd just been the messenger who had to deliver the bad news. Hopefully that also meant she'd deliver good news, too, when she had healthy livestock for him. Even if it was camels or kangaroos.

"Sure," he said instead, crossing his fingers that it wouldn't be camels.

THREE

It wasn't long before Rana found herself cursing Ira, Paris, and her own strict criteria for what they should do for a celebration of the Colony's first birthday. By the time her meeting with Ira rolled around, she was almost ready to curse the Colony so it never made it to its first anniversary, let alone another one. But that wouldn't be fair. This had been the most peaceful year she could remember for a long time. She hadn't feared for her life for a single day in the Colony. And that was worth celebrating.

So when she marched into Ira's office, she didn't let him say a word before she launched into her plans.

"I want to link our celebration with Earth, so at first I looked at holidays they celebrated in the past. Things that were shared by more than one culture, that could still be relevant, light years away, centuries into the future," she began. "Only one celebration ticked every box on my list: an ancient North American holiday they called Thanksgiving. It had its own historical roots in harvest festivals, thanking various deities for a successful harvest, but it's also about a new colony, struggling to get started, where the first inhabitants and the new colonists shared a meal, despite fighting over the land. Or at least that's how it started. Over the centuries, it changed to being about family, and community, and sharing a meal, usually of several specific foods, which changed over time. And being thankful for things, and people." Rana took a deep breath. "That's why I think we should call this Thanksgiving, a celebration of everyone working together to build a better world than the ones we left behind, like it said in the advertising for the Colony. A grand public event with food and music, in some of the big plazas in Metropolis City, where everyone is invited."

Ira's face lit up with a rare, genuine smile. "Rana, you are truly a pearl beyond price. Whatever I'm paying you, you should double it."

She'd already done that at the beginning of the week, on his orders, but she wasn't going to complain about doing it again. "I'll sort the paperwork and have it on your desk to sign by Monday morning."

Ira nodded. "So what sort of food is traditional at a Thanksgiving dinner?"

Stars, she'd seen so many things, depending on the date and country, which were more about what was available at the time, because that's how it worked with harvest feasts. "I'm going to make a list, then cross reference it with what we currently have available, or can create here in the Colony, then check it against the dietary requirements for the people here, to make sure we have something for everybody."

Ira rose and rubbed his hands together. "This is starting to sound better and better. I'm sure you have a lot of work to do. Don't let me keep you!" He ushered her out of his office and closed the door.

Rana blinked. That had to be the fastest meeting she'd ever had with Ira. She'd expected to be in his office for hours, fighting over every bit of her plan. He'd agreed to everything, plus finished the meeting before five on a Friday. She might actually be able to go home on time, like a normal person.

No, not might. She would. The dinner

menu could wait until Monday, along with the paperwork for her pay rise, if Ira approved it.

Before Rana could second guess herself, she marched out of the Watch offices, and all the way to the aircar station for her ride home.

FOUR

Normally, Byron shifted the banana pallets to the ripening sheds with the help of the labourers from Farm 1, Nang Tani's banana plantation, when they delivered them. Today, given the labourers were likely back at work on Nang's farm or wherever else they were needed, Byron decided to do them all himself.

About halfway through, he sincerely regretted his decision, but he doggedly continued. What else did he have to do? There were no cows to tend, his house had been left immaculate by the quarantine team, and the sooner he finished, the sooner he'd have fresh, ripe bananas to eat.

He was under no illusions why Nang only allowed him to ripen her bananas. It wasn't because of superior skill or experience, or because he was quicker than the others. Actually, he tended to take more time – a day or even two days longer than most. No, it was because he accepted part payment in bananas, and he prided himself on ripening them perfectly, so that his payment was just right. Oh, and there was the matter of the algae tanks he used to scrub the air clean in the shed, which yielded Nang's favourite seaweed. The Colony had a monetary system like any other world, and the credits were handy when he needed to buy something, but Byron much preferred the barter system. Trading and bargaining were more fun, and there was something about holding your payment in your hand after the trade was done.

Not that Byron would mention that to anybody, or he'd risk being called archaic, which came with a whole lot of other notions he didn't like or agree with in the slightest. He found it hard to believe that people in archaic times had actually believed a person's value was dependent on their sex and skin colour. Someone with that sort of attitude wouldn't last long in the Colony, where Titans could have any skin colour imaginable, and some of them didn't even have a gender. Not to mention that disrespecting a Maintenance worker, no matter what colour or sex they were, was a good way to make sure nothing ever got fixed when you were around.

He'd heard of one labourer whose toilet had been blocked for a solid week, after he'd made an inappropriate comment to the female plumber who'd come to fix it. In the end, he'd had to fix that shit himself.

Byron was pretty sure the plumber had been Allie, who'd installed the algae tanks. She'd spent the whole time singing while she worked, and the cows had congregated outside the sheds to listen, instead of avoiding her like they had most other visitors to the farm. Any girl who could charm cows was all right by him.

Not that he had any cows to charm now, nor was he likely to have any in the near future, either.

A chime rang through the farm, telling him someone was waiting at the entrance. Likely Nang, wanting to know when her bananas would be ready.

As he approached, the door slid open.

"Doctor Lilith," he said in surprise.

"Mr Kidd." She cleared her throat. "I know I told you earlier that we'd have to test all the embryos to see if any were viable, and that it would take some time, but it turns out one of our bioengineers, unbeknown to me, had taken it upon himself to improve on our livestock, and to see if he could match the accelerated growth rates someone had introduced into several of the aquaculture species. His first successful experiment reached term in 96 days, which was…yesterday." She didn't look too pleased at this.

Byron took a minute to let her words sink in. "You mean…I might be able to have cows again, soon?" He didn't dare let himself hope.

"Sooner than you think. All experimental animals in Eden are sent to a suitable habitat as soon as they're old enough, and Rocail insists BSE-1 here's suitable habitat is an arid rangeland farm. Yours." Doctor Lilith waved a small floating pallet forward. "Rocail sent enough powdered concentrate to feed her for a week. Four-hourly feeds, to allow for the accelerated growth rate. Next week, you're to vary feeds between pellets and milk..."

Byron didn't need to listen to the rest. He knew how to raise poddy calves — he'd bottle fed every one of the herd he'd lost. He dropped to his knees and peered into the crate.

Dark, long-lashed eyes blinked back at him.

A brand new calf.

Byron took a deep, shaky breath. "Hello, Bessie. Welcome home."

He was in love.

FIVE

Pumpkin pie, mashed potatoes, cranberries, cider, mushy peas…no matter which time period she looked at, she could arrange whatever fruit, vegetables and grains she wished, and anything that relied on those ingredients could be made in large enough quantities to feed the entire Colony population.

Meat, on the other hand…

Rana sighed. The meat that popped up most often in menus throughout the ages was turkey. She'd had to look it up, and found a large bird that hadn't been considered necessary in the Titan colony. Chickens and ducks and various pollinators, yes, but not these monstrosities. She'd had to look in the *Genesis* databases to find out anything about turkeys.

But while she might know what one looked like, finding one would prove harder still. The databases had information about all the plants and animals currently being cultivated in the fledgeling farms throughout the Colony, but turkeys weren't anywhere on that list.

Her only other option was to contact

the bioengineers in Eden, and hope they could give her a turkey. Well, ideally a whole flock, as tradition called for the bird to be stuffed and roasted whole, after which the stuffing was extracted from its nether regions and eaten. Just the thought of it made her shudder.

She didn't have to eat it, or watch other people eat it. All she had to do was make sure it was there for those who could stomach such things.

So she commed Eden.

"Eden Bioengineering Laboratories, Orel speaking. How may I help you?"

"I need a turkey," Rana blurted out.

"I'm sorry…you need what?"

Briefly, Rana explained what she needed and why.

"I'll put you through to Metis. She's

our information officer — if anyone can find what you need, it's Metis."

Rana had only a few seconds to hope and maybe pray before Metis answered, and she had to explain her quandary again.

Metis paused for only a moment, before she said, "I have your search results. We have turkey embryos in stasis, but none currently in production or in the biomes. If you put in a priority request, it's possible we could have your birds in production within a few months, and in sufficient numbers for the second anniversary celebration. But two weeks…I couldn't even get you a tissue sample big enough for vat grown meat in that time. If you'd like emu, though, we have a small flock of those. Not enough to slaughter for meat, of course, but mature enough that you could obtain a sufficiently large tissue sample to start cloning. If you used all the vats in the Colony, you might be able to clone enough emu meat in time."

Rana was almost afraid to ask. "What in the stars is an emu?"

Metis sent her a picture, and Rana had to smother a cry of horror. How could a bird grow as big as a man? If something that huge flew over, nothing would be safe.

"No, thank you," Rana managed to say. "I'll keep looking, and hope I find something else suitable. There had to be a time when roasted, stuffed birds weren't available."

She ended the call, then buried her

face in her hands.

Stars, she wished she'd never agreed to organise this Thanksgiving celebration. She'd be thankful when it was over, and even more thankful if she never had to run an event, EVER again.

When Rana mustered the fortitude to open her eyes again, she crossed turkey off her menu and looked at some of the other things that had been eaten at the earliest documented Thanksgiving celebrations. In America, they'd had fish, which she knew she could easily obtain from the Mer community in the Aqua Dome.

But for those who wanted meat, a traditional part of most Thanksgiving celebrations…

The very first one, a brief meal shared

by a ship's crew upon reaching land in the Arctic in the Earth year of 1578, had included mushy peas, some horrible early version of ration bars they'd called ship's biscuit, and preserved beef. Further research told her beef came from cows, one of the first livestock animals to be introduced to Colony farms.

In fact…Farm 3, Lower Level, Arena Dome had exactly what she needed, right now.

Rana rose from her desk, triumph flowing through her. She could just comm the farm, like she had Eden, but she'd been cooped up in the office all day, and she could do with some exercise.

Besides, she'd never seen a cow before, and she wanted to.

Ah, but first things first. She put in a request for an abattoir drone to be sent to the farm, ready for her arrival. If she only had two weeks, she had no time to lose.

SIX

Bessie, as Byron soon found out, drank like a fish and bounced around her enclosure with so much energy, he'd begun to wonder if the bioengineers had given him a creature that was part kangaroo. Could a bioengineer actually do that? He remembered seeing some old movies back on Earth where bioengineers brought back dinosaurs that were part frog, but that was fiction, and ancient fiction at that.

Whatever else she was, though, Bessie was definitely a cow. And while he wanted a whole herd, he'd happily start with just the one.

While she gambolled and jumped, he sat on the railing with a coil of rope in his hand, throwing a lasso at the opposite fence post, high above her head. He hadn't practiced at all while the ranch was under quarantine, as there had hardly been enough space to swing his arms out wide in his box of an apartment, let alone a rope, and he'd grown rusty. Now, after about half an hour of growing accustomed to the gentle tug of low gravity on the rope, he found he could snag the fence post on almost every try.

Lassoing Bessie as she zoomed around wasn't on the cards for today.

The timer on his wrist beeped – time to feed Bessie again. He hung his rope on the fence post, slid down to the ground, and headed inside to mix her a batch of milk.

He measured out the scoops of powder, shaking the bottle continuously all the way back to Bessie.

A strange buzzing sound made him stop and look up.

"What the…"

Byron dropped the milk bottle and seized the rope, swinging it around his head before letting it go. In Earth gravity, it would have dropped neatly over the top of that flying saucer and let him drag it away from Bessie.

But in the Colony's lighter gravity, the rope soared right over the top of the saucer and hit the fence before dropping to the ground like a dead snake.

Bessie didn't even react. That flying menace had already done something to her, freezing her in place in the beam of light coming out the bottom of it.

Byron saw red. Snatching up the rope as fast as he could coil it, he shouted. "Oi! No alien's abducting my cattle – go get your own livestock. I'm a cowboy from Earth, and last time it was cowboys against aliens, it didn't go well for the aliens. So fly back where you came from, before I make you regret it!"

Finally, he had the rope ready to throw

again. Byron didn't hesitate. This time, he didn't miss, either, tightening the lasso around the top of the saucer before he yanked it toward him.

That's when the alien appeared out of thin air.

SEVEN

Rana had planned to stay in her true, elemental form, instead of the body she wore to the office. She watched the drone chase the cow – which was much smaller than she'd thought it would be – around its enclosure before finally managing to immobilise it, and then he'd shown up.

He could have stepped out of a picture from the archives about some of the earlier Thanksgiving celebrations. The tight blue pants that showed off his butt to perfection, the hat that appeared to be made out of actual cowhide, or something closely synthesised to look like it, and when he drew his arm back to twirl the rope, the way his arm muscles bunched up…she wanted to wrap her hand around them and squeeze…

It took her a moment to realise she'd already started taking form. Two arms, two legs and a head, like the silvery rag dolls made out of insulation foil she'd seen some of the Human refugee children holding. Her first thought was to dematerialise immediately, but the man was looking at her, shouting something as he dragged the drone, now snared in the rope, along the ground behind him.

The little cow had gone back to its previous pastime of running around its enclosure.

Rana cursed quietly under her breath and focussed on finishing the transformation. She was going to have beef at this celebration, and this archaic man with his muscly arms, no matter how lickable, was not going to get in her way.

As always, the last Human sense to reach her brain was hearing, so it wasn't until she stood as tall as he did that she could make sense of what he was shouting at her.

"…you get back in your flying saucer

and fly right out of here, because you are not touching my Bessie!" he finished, breathing hard.

Rana blinked. He stood only a couple metres in front of her, both hands on his hips, with the drone on the ground at his feet.

If anything, it only made his arms look more muscly, like they were strong enough to hold her up while she wrapped her legs around his waist and…

Rana blushed silver. She'd barely been in a Human form for a minute and already she was thinking about sex. Stupid Human hormones. She'd be in more control of them in an hour or two, but right now…

He pointed at the door to the farm habitat. "I said out!"

As a member of the Watch, even if she was just the Commander's Executive Assistant, she had the authority to go anywhere in the Colony for Watch business. She considered telling Mr Muscles this, but she suspected he was angry enough to pick her up and carry her out the door. Worse, if he did, she was certain she'd enjoy it.

Instead, Rana cleared her throat and managed a small smile. "Sir, I'm Rana Eteri from the Watch. I've been ordered to source food supplies from various farms throughout the Colony for the anniversary celebration in two weeks' time. My records show that your farm has the only cow…"

"You're not taking Bessie anywhere, and you're not touching her, either! So take your flying saucer..." Mr Muscles kicked the drone.

"Please don't damage the drone, sir, or I will have to fine you for damage to Colony property," Rana said. And then she'd have to send for another drone, and this would take longer...

"I'll do more than damage it, if it tries to kill my cow again," he said.

Rana blinked. "Sir, I assure you the drone is not here to kill or otherwise injure your cow. It's here to acquire a tissue sample it can take back to the cloning vats in the abattoir, in order to produce enough vat grown beef for the celebration. We need enough beef to serve to everyone in the city and your little cow there wouldn't feed a single dome, let alone the whole Colony."

He stared at her, wonder in his eyes like he was seeing her for the first time. "How big a tissue sample? If you hurt her…"

"I don't know how large it has to be, but I do know that the drone is programmed to anaesthetise the creature and take the sample, without harming the creature. It shouldn't even feel it." Rana scrunched up her nose. "What kind of culture hurts animals? Even when they were slaughtered for meat back on Tito, death was instant and painless, with no unnecessary cruelty. Are Humans on Earth still so barbaric that you would do such a thing?"

Mr Muscles bridled. "I would never hurt one of my herd. Look, miss…"

"My name is Rana Eteri," she offered.

"Miss Eteri...seriously, your name is Mystery?" Mr Muscles' whole demeanour changed when he laughed.

Now she wanted to climb him like a tree.

Oh, stars...

She swallowed. "My name is Rana Eteri. Everyone just calls me Rana."

He smiled and held out his hand. "Rana Eteri, I'm pleased to meet you. I'm Byron Kidd, the farmer in charge of this ranch, and this here's Bessie." He waved in the direction of the cow.

Stars, if she touched him...but she'd have to, wouldn't she? Shaking hands was an old Human custom. She stretched out her trembling fingers and his hand engulfed hers. Rough and calloused, like he'd spent most of his time working with them. Idly, she wondered what that roughness would feel like, rubbing against her most tender parts…

"So, you need to take a tissue sample?"

She blinked. She'd been lost in a daydream…and she still held his hand! She released him. "Yes. If you'll release the drone, please, Mr Kidd, I'll just take that sample and go, like you said."

Go and take a long, cold shower, though he didn't need to know that.

"Byron," he corrected her. "If I can call you Rana, you should call me Byron. Or Billy, if you want. It's what everyone else calls me, on account of the hat." He flicked it with his finger.

She wasn't sure what to say. This was evidently a Human cultural reference that hadn't yet come up in her research. If there was a way she could politely access the network…

He must have seen the look of confusion on her face, because he continued, "Billy the Kid? The cowboy from the movies?" Byron sighed. "I guess aliens don't watch movies, or at least not the same ones."

"Actually, I spend a lot of my evenings watching films. I tend to prefer my favourites from Tito, though." None of which he'd know, being a Human and all. "I shall endeavour to explore Human culture in my evening entertainment in the future."

He grinned. "Actually, there was another movie that started that way. Aliens watching a show they thought were historical documents, who came to Earth to ask for the help of some hero who was actually only an actor…but I guess you haven't seen that one, either."

Rana shook her head. "I'm not an alien. Well, no more an alien than you are, as neither Humans or Titans are from Altan originally. I'm a sylph." From his confused expression, she realised it was her turn to explain. "A sort of air elemental, but we spend a lot of time in a Human-like form. Like this." She waved down at her body, which was now perfectly proportioned, if silver instead of normal Human flesh tone.

"And a very lovely form it is. Uh…" Byron coughed, staring down at his boots, but not fast enough to hide his rosy blush.

"May I…" she began.

At exactly the same moment he said, "Would you like…"

They both laughed.

"You first," he said.

She inclined her head. "May I take the tissue sample so we can start the cloning process?"

His mouth quirked. "You may, Miss Eteri. Actually, it's feeding time for Bessie, so after you've taken your sample, would you like to give her some milk?"

Milk? She glanced down. Human females could lactate, so if she modified the mammary glands, and added nipples, she might be able to… Rana cupped her breasts in her hands and concentrated.

"Stars, not like that! I didn't mean…" Now his face was fiery red. "I make up a special blend of powdered nutrients with water, so it's like milk, and feed it to her from a bottle. No need for breasts of any kind. Though yours are…very nice, beautiful, bountiful even, I'm sure."

Rana couldn't help but feel sorry for the man. "How about I take the sample, and as thanks for your assistance in feeding the Colony, I help you feed your cow?"

"Sounds like we have a deal, Miss Eteri." He stuck out that distractingly, delightfully rough hand.

This time she didn't hesitate to take it. "Absolutely," she said.

EIGHT

This had to be the weirdest day of his life, Byron thought as he released the flying saucer…no, the drone, that's what she'd called it. He still wasn't sure what had possessed him to invite the alien girl to feed Bessie, either. The figure he'd first seen, resembling a small grey alien from any one of a number of old movies, had repulsed him instantly. But when she'd taken a more Human form, and he'd seen her skin go all silvery, he hadn't been able to stop thinking about how pretty she was. Not that thinking was easy, what with her so naked and all…

Byron swallowed. If he squinted a little, he could almost imagine she was wearing a silver coverall. A coverall that clung to every curve, moving smoothly as she did…

No, that wasn't helping.

Bessie. He should think about Bessie.

He reached the calf before the drone did, reaching out to pat her. Bessie, knowing it was feeding time, started sucking on his hand.

The drone buzzed over his head, and

Byron tensed. It hovered over Bessie for a long moment, then rose into the air and flew away. The whole time, Bessie didn't stop sucking on his hand, blissfully unaware of the drone.

"I believe you forgot this?" Rana appeared beside him, shaking the milk bottle.

Bessie's eyes widened and she let go of his hand, stretching for the bottle.

Byron reached for it, helping Rana tip it and guide it into the calf's mouth.

"Hold tight to it, now, or she'll steal it from you," Byron warned, tightening his own grip on the bottle. His fingers brushed hers and he looked up in surprise.

He hadn't realised how close she stood. She smelled like the breeze after a fresh summer rain. All flowers and life and warmth and sweetness…

Stars, but she tasted sweet, too. All sweetness and light, like he couldn't get enough of her. He wanted…

Bessie bawled and butted him through the fence.

Byron tore his lips away from Rana's, his breath leaving him in a shocked gasp. He hadn't meant to touch her, let alone kiss her, and yet…

Rana licked her lips, her eyes on the ground, where the empty bottle had fallen. "I'm sorry, I didn't mean to…"

No, he was sorry. "I shouldn't have. I don't know what…" he said, then broke off.

They both laughed, nervously.

"You're welcome to come back here

any time," he said.

At the same time as she said, "Can I do that again?" She sounded a little breathless.

Bessie wouldn't need feeding again for a few more hours, but… "Sure," he said.

She threw her arms around his neck and kissed him.

It took him a moment to recover from the shock before he could kiss her back, this time conscious of his actions. How her lips were warm against his, her tongue welcoming him, all the while tasting sweet and fresh like no woman he'd ever kissed before.

He didn't want it to end.

He closed his eyes as he felt her pull away from him, breaking the bond between them.

"Thanks," she said.

He opened his eyes, only to find she'd vanished, leaving nothing but the lingering taste of paradise on his tongue.

"You're welcome, any time," he said to the empty air.

NINE

Days passed, but Rana never returned. Bessie grew like a weed, so it was a relief when a shipment of fresh feed pellets arrived for her, along with a lot more powdered milk. Still no Rana, though.

He must have misread the signals somehow, Byron decided as he shifted the now ripe bananas out of the shed.

They'd kissed – twice – and he'd invited her to come back, something she'd seemed eager to do, but…nothing.

Byron sighed. He'd never had any trouble attracting or associating with women when he'd been back on Earth, but since his parents died, he'd been poor company and he hadn't really felt like making the effort any more.

Yet now…here on New Hope, that moment with Rana, he'd dared to hope, and he'd be damned if he gave up on her that easily. He must have messed up without realising, what with being so out of practice getting along with anyone.

Was he supposed to contact her, or something, and invite her over, maybe? Or was it because she was an alien, who expected different things to a Human woman? Maybe there was some alien mating custom he'd never heard of, and wouldn't know, that he'd somehow neglected.

That was probably it. Which meant his best bet was to head into the city, find her, apologise to her and explain that he was just a farm boy from Earth who'd lost the farm there, so he was bumbling his way around a second chance here in space. If she'd give him a second chance, too, that would just be wonderful.

Fat chance of that, if he'd royally stuffed up and she never wanted to see him again. But maybe, just maybe, if he brought her a gift, something really special…

Flowers weren't available for love or money in the Colony, so those were out, and the price of chocolates from the one shop that made them by hand with the experimental cocoa beans that were just coming up to their first harvest…well, it was more credits than he saw in a year.

He needed something bright and sweet that she'd find hard to get anywhere else…inspiration hit him like a charging bull. Yes. Perfect.

When he'd finished working for the day, he changed into a clean shirt and jeans. On impulse, he stuck his hat on his head, too – just in case she didn't remember him, she'd definitely remember the hat.

He'd already checked her office address, so he knew Rana worked at the Watch Headquarters building in Metropolis City. He couldn't remember the last time he'd been into the city — aside from when his ranch was under quarantine, he rarely left it — so he was surprised to see every screen and window advertising the Thanksgiving Festival Rana had spoken about. He'd imagined something small, not a Colony-wide celebration where the entire population was expected to come together in the main squares of the city. Food, drink, entertainment…this was massive.

Bessie would have to do without him for a few hours, because there was no way Byron intended to miss the festival. Especially if he got to see Rana there.

Though she'd likely ignore him if he'd offended her, so he'd best start make amends as early as possible. The sooner the better.

He quickened his steps, his heart beating faster at the thought of seeing her again.

TEN

"Thank you," Rana said and ended the call. Then she blew out a breath and buried her face in her hands. Being an events organiser was the most exhausting job in the world. Why, if Ira were here now, she'd tell him she'd had enough and ask him to find someone else for the job. If she'd had her usual job to do as well, she'd have gone certifiably mad.

But she couldn't tell Ira anything – he'd decided to take a couple of weeks' leave, blocking all work-related communication from his comm chip and his tablet, and leaving his office empty. After the first day of fielding all manner of enquiries about Ira's whereabouts, she'd abandoned her own desk and retreated behind the closed door of his office. Anyone who'd dared to open that door soon found themselves conscripted into helping her with the Thanksgiving Festival, so they'd quickly learned to leave her alone.

Of course, she still had Festival business to handle, so her comm chip was rarely silent. One call would end, but a moment later, someone else would…

Knock, knock, knock.

Rana blinked. No one knocked on the door.

"Er…come in?" she suggested.

The door slowly opened, and a head appeared in the gap.

"Byron!" she exclaimed. Rana jumped to her feet, rounded the desk, and practically threw herself into his arms. Her lips were on his before her brain had truly caught up with her body.

By the time it did, all she could think about was how good his arms felt around her, and stars, how well the man could kiss…

She was panting when she finally managed to pry herself away from him, and not without considerable regret.

He looked flustered. "Uh, hi. I didn't

realise you were one of the high-ups in the Watch. I mean, I should've guessed, seeing as how big your event is, but I've been busy on the ranch and…stars, you look beautiful in uniform." Byron swallowed.

Rana glanced down. Somehow, her shirt buttons had come undone and her breasts were all but popping out. Not that she minded getting naked around Byron – she'd been naked when they met, after all – but something like archaic Earth chivalry had him averting his gaze from her.

"I'm not high up at all. I'm just an assistant. It's my boss who's important. The office is his. Usually, I'm the dragon on the desk outside, guarding the door. I'm not even really a Watch officer, but the uniform is expected during work hours, so, for another…" She glanced at the time, and her eyes widened in surprise. "Actually, my work day is officially over, so I'm allowed to get out of uniform." It was her turn to swallow. "If you'd like."

From the heated look in his eyes and the way he started to nod, she knew he'd definitely like.

As for Rana herself, well…she could hardly blame being in a Human form this time. She burned for him, more fiercely than when they'd first kissed. She wanted Byron, right here, right now.

He held up a bag. "I brought you a present."

She couldn't remember the last time a man had brought her a gift. Impossibly, her desire burned hotter.

She took the bag from him and peered inside, then stared at him in puzzlement. Why would he give her a yellow severed hand?

"They're bananas, fresh from the farm," he explained. "Most of the crop goes to high-end restaurants and cafes, or to the richer colonists, who can afford luxuries like fresh fruit. I always keep a portion for myself, and I thought...I thought you might like to try them, if you haven't had bananas before."

Stars bless him, she was in love with this thoughtful man. If she hadn't wanted to get naked before...

"I've never seen a banana before," she admitted.

"Then let me show you," he said

eagerly, snapping one of the fat fingers off what she'd thought was a hand. He peeled it open like some exotic flower, revealing the soft, creamy flesh inside. He held it out. "Taste it."

Cautiously, she stuck her tongue out and licked the tip. Yes, it was soft, and a little sweet.

"Please," Byron implored her.

Rana took a deep breath, opened her mouth wide, and took a huge bite. Sweetness exploded on her tongue, her mouth so full it took an effort to swallow. But she did, because she wanted more.

She could hear someone moaning, and it took her a moment to realise it was her. Moaning in pleasure at a piece of fruit, for stars' sake.

Then her eyes met Byron's, and she forgot the fruit altogether.

Her lips fused to his, in a kiss so perfect, she swore time stopped.

Somehow her shirt had come open completely, giving him all the access he needed to caress her breasts with both hands, followed by his tongue. She leaned back, gripping the desk behind her so she didn't topple over, moaning anew at the pleasure of his touch.

He pressed against her, so all she could feel was hard muscle, all the way down.

She needed her pants off, now. Hers and his. But she didn't want him to take his hands off her breasts, so she'd have to do this herself. Without looking down, because he was kissing her again, his tongue dancing with hers, and she had no intention of breaking this kiss.

Ever…

Only the crash of someone slamming the door open could part her from Byron, and only because Byron had the fortitude to pull away.

"Rana, have you seen that book I borrowed? That girl at the library is demanding that I return it before I borrow another one, and I can't find it anywhere!"

She'd never wanted to kill her boss quite as much as she did now, eyeing daggers at his back as he surveyed the shelves around his office, unaware of what he'd interrupted or even that she wasn't alone. Of course, that did give her a moment to button up her shirt before she slid off the desk, to reveal the paperback she'd been sitting on.

"You mean this book, sir?" she asked, holding it up.

Ira snatched it out of her hand. "Yes! Now Hestia will have to let me have a new book." He stalked out, slamming the door behind him.

Byron let out a shaky breath. "Maybe we should…go somewhere else? I could…take you out for dinner or something?"

What she wanted more than anything was to go somewhere with him where they could finish what they'd started on Ira's desk, without being interrupted. But she had too much work to do.

Perhaps after the Festival…

Rana sighed. "I can't. I have to work.

This stars-crossed Festival. There's so much more to do, and not enough time." Her eyes begged him to forgive her.

He bowed his head. "I understand. Perhaps after the Festival…"

"Definitely." The word was out of her mouth before she could think. "You are coming to the Festival, aren't you?"

"Of course. That's…that's what I came here to ask you. If you'd come to the Festival with me, as my date," he said.

Gifts and kissing and fruit and dates? Rana felt dizzy. "Yes," she breathed. "Yes, I'd love to be your date."

He smiled. "I'll pick you up here at six on Friday, then?"

"Yes." And on Friday, she'd make sure she wasn't wearing any pesky pants.

Even if she had to comb the whole Colony for a suitable Festival dress.

Byron took off his hat, and bowed. "Until Friday, then."

For the first time in her life, Rana almost swooned. By the time she'd recovered, he was gone.

It didn't matter, she told herself. She'd see him at the Festival on Friday, and afterwards, she'd have a whole weekend without work or interruptions to do whatever she wished.

ELEVEN

Time alternated between flying and crawling until finally it was Friday, and Byron headed back to the Watch headquarters building. Just like before, he told the receptionist he was there to see Rana Eteri, and was soon headed up in the elevator to the top floor.

This being a Watch office, he wasn't

surprised to see several uniformed officers along the way, but he paid them little attention. His only thoughts were for Rana and how much he wanted to make this evening special for her.

He glanced at the desk outside the office she'd been in last time, which was surrounded by Watch officers, all wearing the same uniform. None of them had her silvery skin, though.

"Is that him? He really is a cowboy!" one officer said, staring at Byron.

"Nice hat," said another officer.

Byron grinned. He was pretty sure it was the only genuine leather cowboy hat in the whole Altan system. "That it is," he drawled, tipping it at the man who'd complimented him.

"Don't you all have work to do?" Rana

scolded.

As if by some alien magic, the crowd parted.

And there she was, casting her alien spell over him again. She wasn't wearing the Watch uniform – instead, she wore a dress made of some fabric he fancied was almost see-through, fluttering in the slight air current from the ventilation units, giving him a tantalising glimpse before the floating feathers of fabric settled so thickly again they hid her skin from sight.

Off came the hat. Byron bowed low, offering her his arm. "You're so blindingly beautiful, you'd make the whole galaxy of stars jealous. I bet there are nebulae out in the sky right now, conspiring to copy your dress, and you'll still outshine them."

Rana blushed silver. "That might just be the loveliest compliment anyone's ever given me."

"Every word is the truth, I swear."

The officer who'd called him a cowboy folded her arms across her chest as she narrowed her eyes at him. "Just because he can string a few pretty words together, doesn't make him a good man. You want me to run a background check for you, Rana? If he's on our wanted list, better if I handcuff him now." She jingled the cuffs on her belt.

Rana shooed the officer away. "I'll be fine, Minali. No handcuffs required. We're going to the Festival." She laid her hand on Byron's arm, and her touch sent an electrical pulse crackling straight to his brain. Which then sent blood rushing other places…

Byron cleared his throat and tried to think of something cold. Prison cells, shackles, space… There. That got things under control. "Shall we?"

With Rana on his arm, the two of them marched out of the Watch building.

"Where would you like to go for dinner? The food's supposed to be the same all over, but the drinks are provided by the individual businesses closest to the tables. So, the Moon and Sixpence tables will have the best beer, Forge does the best cocktails, and I forget what the wine bar's called, but if fermented grape juice is your thing…" Rana trailed off, her eyes enquiring.

"What do you want to drink?" Byron asked. He didn't care, as long as she was happy.

Another silver blush. "After the bananas you brought me, I went looking for more fruit, and discovered a juice bar over by the lake. They make this delightful drink they tell me is called a margarita, a mix of ice and fruit and fire, or at least that's what it tastes like."

Byron hadn't had a margarita since he'd been on Earth. "A table by the lake, then, and margaritas for us both," he said.

A table for two would have been best, but this was a festival for the whole Colony, so they found themselves on the end of a long trestle table full of all kinds of people. Some Human, and some definitely alien. Rana earned a few stares, particularly from the Humans, but Byron wasn't sure if it was the colour of her skin or her stunning dress that had everyone looking. Or maybe they just saw what he did – how beautiful she was.

A waitress came to take their order.

"Two margaritas, and two standard menus," Rana said, before Byron could even open his mouth.

The waitress hurried off.

"What if I wanted to order something special, not on the standard menu?" he asked carefully.

Rana's eyes widened in surprise. "Then you'd get it, of course, but whether you'd want to eat it is another matter. Thank the stars food allergies are a thing of the past, but some Titans can't stomach steak and mashed potato and pumpkin pie and…I forget the rest. Oh, there's fish, of course, and we do have some vegetarians, but the vampires and a few others prefer blood. The elementals have their own preferences, and don't forget the dryads…"

Byron's jaw dropped. How many kinds of aliens were there in the Colony? He needed to get out more. "Steak and mash and pumpkin pie sound wonderful," he assured her, then perked up. "Hey, is that the vat beef grown from Bessie?"

Rana beamed. "It sure is. Thanks to you and Bessie, the whole Colony can celebrate Thanksgiving with steak. Quite an improvement over ration bars or whatever historic Humans had at their Thanksgiving feasts, all those centuries ago."

He took her hand. "And the company here is infinitely better, too."

Another blush. "If you flatter me too much, my face is going to ache from smiling by the end of the night."

"If that's your only complaint about our night together, I'll be delighted," he said.

Their food arrived then and they were soon busy, cutting and tasting the food.

Byron couldn't smother a moan at the first taste of steak. The last time he'd had steak this good, his mother had cooked it. This, however, melted on his tongue.

"Is it good?" Rana asked anxiously.

Byron swallowed, trying to think of the right superlatives to make her understand it was better than good. Just short of pure, carnal heaven.

"Excuse me, Miss Eteri?" a waitress asked.

Rana looked up. "Yes?"

"There's been an altercation between the proprietor of the Moon and Sixpence and the owner of the Chocolaterie. Neither can agree on the boundary for drink service and even though there are Watch officers there, they aren't certain, either. One of them said to ask you, because neither of them will back down until they get a ruling from you in person."

Rana rose. "I'm so sorry, Byron. Do you mind if I go sort this out? I'll be right back."

He did his best to hide his disappointment behind a cheerful smile.

"I'll guard your seat while you're gone. But if you take too long, and your steak starts looking mighty tempting, I will not be held responsible if it goes missing."

She thanked him and hurried away.

Ten minutes passed, then twenty. An hour later, after he'd finished his dinner and dessert, her plate still sat there, untouched. He sent her a comm message, saying he'd surrendered to temptation and stolen her steak, so she'd have to come back and arrest him. Another hour passed, but still she didn't return, and he didn't receive a reply, either.

Finally, Byron was forced to admit defeat. The date had ended in disaster, and she'd decided not to come back. He couldn't stay any longer, anyway — he needed to feed Bessie.

Music rang out across the plaza, coming from various stages set up all over the place. He squeezed through a group of dancers, heading for the aircar station. He wasn't in the mood for dancing tonight. Not without Rana.

Bessie was waiting for him, letting him know in no uncertain terms that she was hungry and unhappy he'd made her wait.

"Sorry, honey. There was a party in town, and I thought it would be fun to go," he said. "I won't make that mistake again. I'll be right back with your milk." He headed inside.

No, he wouldn't be making that mistake again.

TWELVE

The boundary issue was one of half a dozen across the city, all requiring her personal attention, and when she was done dealing with those, an argument had broken out in the vampire bar over payment for blood. She'd made arrangements for a tab of sorts, enough for every vampire, strigoi or other listed blood drinker to have a free meal, but once they'd reached the total, they'd have to start paying for their drinks, like everyone else. It didn't help that some of the patrons had been drinking more than blood tonight, and were rather belligerent toward the bartender, who'd had to call in the Watch…

By the time Rana had a moment to even look at her messages, Byron was long gone. A family of shifters were sitting in their seats, and there was no sign of him. Rana wanted to cry.

But she took a deep breath, then stripped off her dress, and handed it to the nearest Watch officer, with orders to get it back to her office. Then, air elemental that she was, she took to the air. Or, more accurately, the ventilation ducts.

When her feet formed in the warm sand of Byron's farm, it was like coming home. Bessie the calf even bawled a greeting at her. Or maybe the little cow was hungry, seeing as Byron didn't seem to be here.

Her heart constricted in her chest. Maybe he'd decided to stay at the Festival, and celebrate with someone else, instead of waiting for her. She could hardly blame him. Even now, he might be dancing the night away in a club like Forge, which had advertised a special performance from Vulcan, who usually only performed there at New Year's Eve.

Bessie bawled again, more insistently.

"It's all right, girl. He can dance all he likes. I'll feed you, and then I'll go home to bed. Best place for me, after the night I've had," Rana said, turning toward the house.

Only to come face to face with Byron, holding a bottle of milk in each hand. Wearing nothing but a pair of tight shorts that covered the essentials. Covered and outlined them in glorious detail, hiding nothing.

It was enough to make her want to cry.

"I'm sorry," she began, then couldn't seem to find the words to continue.

"So am I," he said in the silence. "I tried to take you out to dinner, and I didn't even manage that. I figured if I fed Bessie, then maybe one girl wouldn't go hungry tonight. I've got food in the house, if you want me to make you something."

She waved away his offer. "Air elemental. I don't really need food. I get all the energy I need from riding the air currents in the ventilation system. Only if I stay in a corporeal form for more than a day or so, then I need to eat something. So, I won't need anything until breakfast."

He nodded. "I heard you say you wanted a bed. Plenty of those in the house, too. Then I could make you breakfast in the morning, to make up for tonight."

Her heart melted. "You've got nothing to make up for. You were wonderful. It's me, I shouldn't have left you like that. If anything, I'm the one who should apologise, to make it up to you for such a dull evening. Stars, the only thing getting me through this crazy week was the thought of spending the night with you at the end of it, and fantasising about the sex we'd have. Now..." She shook her head.

Byron set the milk down and held up his hands. "Now, hold on a minute. Did you just say you've been thinking about me all week?"

She felt a blush heating her cheeks. How did he do this to her so often? "Well, yes, in between wishing I could forget about this Festival altogether. I guess now it's over, and I have the whole weekend to myself, I can forget about it. Or at least try."

"You could spend your weekend here. Maybe I could show you some of the

Human films about aliens, and you can show me some of your favourite ones from Tito."

All that sounded very tempting, but it wasn't all that different to what she'd do at home alone. "Will there be sex?" she ventured, hardly daring to hope.

Byron blinked. "Well, there's that scene in *Galaxy Quest* where the guy gets with the alien and she has these tentacles…"

"If you want a form with tentacles, I could try to transform, but I'm not as familiar with krakens as Humans, so I have no idea where their pleasure centres are, if they have any at all. Humans have the most erogenous zones, so I thought this would be the best form for sex." Rana waved at her body, suddenly wishing she'd thought to ask him instead of just assuming. If he wanted tentacles…

"I think your body is perfect just as it is. And tentacles…they can totally wait until our second or third date, maybe. If we make it that far," Byron said.

Rana found herself nodding. It must be some peculiar Human custom not to break out the tentacles on a first date. It seemed perfectly reasonable to her. "Sure. We could – "

Bessie bawled again, even louder.

"Let me just feed the cow, and then I'm all yours," he said.

Oh, now that sounded just wonderful.

"Let me help you," Rana purred.

THIRTEEN

While Rana fed Bessie, Byron couldn't stop staring at her. Rana, not the calf. He knew those margaritas had slowed his wits somewhat, but the thoughts going round and round in his head were getting clearer all the time.

Rana had been thinking about him all week.

She'd fantasised about having sex with him.

Better yet, it wasn't crazy alien tentacle sex – it was the Human on Human variety he knew best.

Of course, there were so many ways two Humans could have sex, so maybe he didn't…

Suddenly he felt a burning urge to know exactly what her fantasies had involved, but his mouth felt too dry to form the words, no matter how many times he swallowed.

Rana turned her shimmering eyes on him, her smile lighting up her whole face. No, the whole universe. "Bessie's fed. Shall we have sex, then?"

"Stars, yes," he swore.

FOURTEEN

Rana wasn't sure how they made it into the house, or where his shorts had vanished, but when they toppled together onto the bed, their lips still locked, she didn't care about anything but Byron and how hot and hard he felt against her. How he'd feel inside her…

He covered her body in kisses, parting

her thighs with both hands so that he might kiss her there, too, lingering long enough to make her squeal out his name for joy.

That's when he looked up at her and grinned, before flopping down on the bed beside her.

"Have you ever ridden a cowboy before, my sexy sylph?" he asked.

Warmth flooded her chest. He'd remembered. "I've never met a cowboy before you," she admitted. "How do I…?"

He helped her sit up and straddle his hips, positioning her just so. Rana could feel the heat of him beneath her, ready for her, and she couldn't resist any longer. She pressed down, letting out a soft moan as he filled her. His hands were hot against her hips as she started to move. No, he started to move, and she moved with him. A slow rise and fall, like riding the breeze, flowing together, part of one being, feeling her pleasure building, her breath quickening, perfectly in time with Byron.

Until she sucked in a lungful of air, teetering on the cliff, before flying over with him, crying out his name, as he roared hers.

It took her several minutes to catch her breath, while pleasure still thrummed through her. She'd never get enough of this, of him. Ever.

"Stars take dates. I don't want them. I want to stay here and have sex with you all weekend," she said, still breathless.

"As long as you want me, I'm all

yours," he promised.

As he began to pleasure her again, her thoughts turned lazily to how they'd come together. How the worst birthday present ever – responsibility for the Thanksgiving Festival – had brought her and Byron together. The universe worked in strange ways, but she was mighty thankful for Byron right now.

Especially when his fingers were…were…and his tongue…

Rana drew in a deep breath, before she screamed for joy.

Ready to spend more time
in the Colony? Read on for
a sneak peek of the next
book, *Ghost*!

ONE

Maia wasn't sure what woke her, but it sure was chilly in the break room tonight. Someone had probably switched off the heating to save power again, forgetting that the night shift nurses napped there when the patient load allowed it. Either that or the old wiring had shorted out again. She'd have to call Maintenance, to make sure they fixed it this time.

Then something touched her tummy, brushing it lightly like a lover might. Problem was, Maia didn't have a lover right now.

"Aren't you a delightful specimen," a male voice crooned.

Her eyes flew open. No one called her a specimen and got away with it.

Definitely not Mr Tall, Dark and Purple, who was staring at her rounded midsection like it was his next meal.

Her breath caught in her throat. Either this was a very unfunny joke, she was hallucinating, or there was an honest to goodness alien standing over her with a syringe.

She squinted at the vial he'd stuck the syringe into. No way was she letting him inject her with a sedative. Stars only knew what he'd done to her before she woke up.

Good thing she'd taken those self defence classes at the hospital back home. The ones for dealing with difficult patients, or particularly violent ones. First she disabled him with a well-placed elbow, before a deft twist transferred the syringe from his hand to hers. She didn't hesitate – she knew a dose meant for her wouldn't kill him. She stabbed the needle deep into his neck and shoved the plunger down until all the liquid was gone.

"Hey, you…" he slurred, twisting away from her before she could take the syringe out. But the sedative was already taking effect, so he slumped over her legs, a dead, drooling weight.

Maia slid out from under him, and hopped off the gurney. It was the high tech sort that could take vital signs continuously – the sort only rich people and private hospitals could afford. And aliens, apparently, or at least whack jobs who liked to colour their skin purple so they looked like aliens. His scrubs had ridden up, so she could see his skin was purple all the way down, not just his face. Weirdo.

She heaved the rest of him onto the gurney, then used the restraints to strap him down, just in case he woke up. Even with her massive belly, she was pretty sure she weighed less than him, so the sedative wouldn't keep him out for long.

Rifling through the cupboards of the medbay, she found herself a set of scrubs, and some more sedative to keep him docile, just in case. Oh, and some spray-on bandage so she could take that needle out of his neck and stem the bleeding. She dressed quickly, then pulled the syringe out. He didn't even wake when the bandage hit his skin, and she knew from experience that stuff stung. He'd meant to knock her out for a while, then.

She wanted to shake him awake and ask him what in the universe he'd thought he was doing to her. Nothing good, that's for sure.

Maia sighed. Whatever it was, she was free now, and he was her prisoner. That had to count for something. But first, she should get a feel for her surroundings, maybe call the police or something. Yes. That would be sensible.

She found an injector gun, and loaded it with sedative. Six doses, for men like the Purple Prick here. Maybe seven if she had to shoot someone her size.

She hoped she wouldn't have to shoot anyone. She'd probably miss, unless it was at point blank range, or whatever you called it when you held a weapon to someone's skin. She was a nurse, not a soldier.

Gripping the injector in both hands, she headed out of the medbay.

Whoever this whack job was, he could certainly afford expensive toys. Sleek, gleaming walls greeted her at every turn, and the seats in his lounge area looked like real leather. She stepped into what could only be called a cockpit and her heart sank. She was in space, judging by how that moon was growing bigger and bigger in the viewscreen. Maybe he was an alien and not a whack job after all.

No, he was an alien whack job, and that was that.

She'd done a cursory search of the living quarters, then a quick glance into the cavernous cargo bay, before she came to the conclusion that she was alone with him on the ship. Well, that made things simpler.

The gurney had a hover capability, which made it easy for her to push all the way from the medbay to the airlock. It could even decant him onto the floor, like a load of dirty laundry. She particularly liked that function.

Gritting her teeth, she dragged the gurney back out in the corridor and closed the airlock, with the alien inside. Then she engaged the manual lock, so he couldn't get out, and sat down to wait.

Loud clanging woke her from her unplanned nap, followed by some particularly colourful swearing. So she had successfully locked him in, then, and he didn't have some secret way out she hadn't been able to find.

She peeked through the little view window. The restraints still held him, and from all the flailing about like a fresh-caught fish, it sounded like he liked being held captive even less than she did. Ah, but he'd spied her, and she was pretty sure fish couldn't feel the sort of fury she saw on his face.

"Foolish woman, I demand you release me immediately, or you'll regret it!" he shouted.

Maia cocked her head to the side. "Mm, no, I don't think I will, thanks. I feel much safer with this big, thick airlock door between us."

He began to struggle again. "Foolish girl! You don't understand. If you don't release me right now, both you and the specimen will die!"

So he wasn't calling her a specimen – he was referring to whatever made her belly so round. Maia's breath caught in her throat at the thought of some alien larva bursting out of her.

"What did you put in me, you prick?" she demanded, before realising that she might have answered her own question. He was an alien, and she did look pregnant...

"You carry within you a child that combines the best of our two species. If he but survives the birth, he will be a god among men. Now, you must release me so I can remove him, before your weak form expires like the other, inferior hosts."

Fury flooded her veins. This arsehole had not only raped and impregnated her, but he'd done the same to other women, before he'd killed them. He deserved to be cut up into little pieces — while he was still alive, of course — and forced to watch them being fed to some primitive predator. A shark, maybe. If only there was a shark tank aboard, but she hadn't seen one. Probably for the best. It'd be a lot of effort and she wasn't sure this arsewipe was worth it.

"We have a name for things like you," she spat. "Psychopath. Or serial killer. Either way, it sounds like the universe will be a better place if I release you out the airlock."

"My name is Kronos, foolish girl, and I am a genius! My experiments will create a super race, formed of Titan and Human, who will rule the universe!"

Maia wasn't sure whether to laugh or cry. Super villain, much?

"Release me, and I will grant you the honour of bearing more of my master race. Generations hence, they will worship you as their mother goddess!"

Being kept in a prison and forced to become a brood mare for this psycho's children? In what universe was that something she could possibly want?

"Sounds like I'll be doing the universe a favour, Purple People Eater," she said, slamming her clenched fist down on the manual release for the outer door.

He let out another stream of curses, higher pitched this time as he started to panic, before he was swept out into space.

Maybe it made her a bit of a psychopath,

too, but Maia couldn't bring herself to regret ridding the universe of one more entitled arsehole. Besides, she had her own problems to deal with, she thought as she glanced down. There was definitely movement in her belly, which couldn't be good.

Time to call an ambulance or the police, if there was such a thing as emergency services in space. Call for help from someone, anyway. And when help was on the way, she'd head back to the medbay and do some scans on herself and her…passenger.

TWO

"No," Nihal said.

Ghost spread his arms wide. "Is that any way to greet your only brother? What would your boss say if he knew you were turning away good customers?"

Nihal yanked a tray of glasses out of the dishwasher and began to put them away. "Vulcan knows as well as I do that you've never been and never will be a paying customer in this place. You only drink cheap beer, and we don't serve that here. You only come in here when you want a favour from me. Last time, you asked me to pick colour schemes for your new house. I nearly went cross eyed, trying to tell the difference between dove grey and mist, or a hundred different shades of white, to pick the perfect one, only to get a completely different palette for the next room. So whatever it is you want, the answer is no."

Ghost knew she couldn't really be serious. They were all the family each other had. "Come on, you know you wanted to decorate my house. I'd have picked one colour and done the whole house in that. See? I saw that shudder. You liked picking out all those colours. But this isn't about my new house. If I can get you to chance your no into a yes, will you give me a drink of the good stuff?"

She sniffed. "That depends. Are you on call tonight?"

Ghost winced. "Yes, but we both know the callout won't come on Christmas Eve. It'll be tomorrow, when we sit down to lunch or dinner. Besides, I've told you before, the alcohol evaporates when I dematerialise. When I arrive where I'm needed and reassemble myself, I'm as sober as the next man."

As if he was secretly trying to prove Nihal's point, the man next to Ghost slipped off his bar stool and crashed to the floor, knocking himself out. The fresh cocktail he'd held in his hand splashed everywhere, soaking Ghost's pants.

The scent of fruit syrup and potent spirits wafted up. Ghost wrinkled his nose.

"I'm not serving alcohol to Emergency Services personnel who are on duty. If you got called in and your slow reflexes got someone killed, I'd never forgive myself," Nihal said. "I'll bet you a virgin mojito you won't change my mind, which means if I win, you buy that drink for me." She grinned.

Ooh, she was twisty. No wonder she was a water djinn, while he was master of the whirlwind instead.

"Deal," Ghost said.

She turned away from him to serve a couple of customers, before she was back. "All right. What is it you want, brother mine?"

"You remember that aircar accident in the tunnels to Nyx last week?"

Nihal frowned. "That was nasty. Didn't a bunch of people end up in hospital? The tunnel was closed for hours – some of our patrons couldn't get home. Did you have to do the cleanup for that?" Something in her expression started to soften.

"I was the first on the scene. The other guys needed to get into their EV suits, but you know me – I head straight in, naked, no suit needed. One aircar had crashed into the other, shattering several of the windows. Rapid decompression and loss of atmosphere, plus damage to the ventilation units, meant a carload of people got decompression sickness, before the safety systems kicked in and sealed the holes. First thing I did was turn up the oxygen levels to maximum, which helped. But one passenger, he was just a kid, a teenager, he had heart problems. That's all he managed to tell me before he passed out. Because I was there first, I could relay to the others we needed emergency evac for him first, and he survived. Wanted to see me today to thank me, in fact. Said I'd saved his life." Ghost grinned. It wasn't often he got to be a hero, but it was an awesome feeling. That was what kept him going, even when his search and rescue callouts didn't have such happy endings.

"So you're a hero. You do a lot of good in Emergency Services, Ghost. Don't let anyone tell you different."

Ghost managed to keep the smile on his face, but it was hard. He didn't want to tell Nihal that he couldn't remember a week when someone hadn't screamed at him for failing to save their partner/child/pet/prized possession when nothing short of a miracle would've saved them, and maybe not even that. Those last days on Tito, when the robot rebellion destroyed half the city, he'd had people screaming at him, blaming him for the deaths he'd arrived too late to prevent. Some of them had actually expected him to run out in front of the robots and get killed trying to retrieve their loved one's corpse. It had been a special kind of hell, working in Emergency Services back then. So for every time he fought fate and failed…it was nice to have the occasional victory. Especially as there were no robots in the Colony at all.

The Colony was also the only place in the whole Altan system with cocoa beans, though the first crop had been very small, and bought in its entirety by one business owner. "Do you know a café owner called Dulcinea?" Ghost asked.

Nihal's eyes widened. "You mean the

woman who owns the Chocolaterie? She comes in here occasionally. She's quite partial to our pomegranate fizz, especially now we can get real pomegranates to garnish the glass."

Ghost nodded. "That's her. Well, the owner of the Chocolaterie, anyway – I don't know what she normally drinks. I do know that she's the relieved mother of Pollux, a teenage boy who's lucky to be alive right now. Relieved and so grateful, in fact, that she said I could come in and choose my favourites to fill her biggest box of truffles to take home. Seeing as you like chocolate so much and your taste is oh so much better than mine…" He suppressed a grin when he saw she at least had the grace to blush. "Well, I thought what better Christmas present for my favourite sister than to ask you to make the selection, so you can enjoy all those chocolates?"

Nihal leaped over the bar and wrapped him in a tight hug. "Yes! A thousand times yes! You are the best brother, Ghost!"

He waited for her to get back behind the bar before he said, "See? I knew you'd say yes. So, does that mean I get that drink? Some sort of virgin, you said?"

Nihal raised her eyebrows. "I didn't think you were into virgins of any kind."

Now it was Ghost's turn to blush. Of course his sister knew he was attracted to women who were a little more experienced, who hadn't lived the most sheltered lives. Stars knew neither of them had been particularly sheltered, even on Titan. Ghost had gotten his taste for cheap beer when that's the best he could afford, and drinking the more expensive stuff seemed like forgetting where he'd come from.

But this wasn't about women. "Make me my drink, woman," he growled.

"If you weren't giving me a big box of chocolates tomorrow, I'd box your ears for that," Nihal said. She reached into the fridge and pulled out a jar of leaves, then plucked several out of the jar.

Ghost couldn't remember the last time he'd smelled fresh mint.

Nihal smiled. "Wait until you taste the syrup. From real Colony honey, harvested in the Ager Dome. The lime juice is still from concentrate, but I hear we'll have our first citrus harvest in a few short months, so it's not long to wait now."

As Ghost watched, she assembled the cocktail, layer by layer, until she reached for the leaf jar again to pluck one more sprig of mint. "For my hero of a brother, who gives the best – "

His comm buzzed.

Ghost's heart tightened in his chest as he read the message. "I'm needed at work. Sorry, sis, I have to go." He gave the drink one last, longing look, before heading for the door.

"I'll put in the fridge for you!" she called after him.

"I'll be back for it!" he called back.

Or so he thought.

ABOUT THE AUTHOR

Demelza Carlton has always loved the ocean, but on her first snorkelling trip she found she was afraid of fish.

She has since swum with sea lions, sharks and sea cucumbers and stood on spray drenched cliffs over a seething sea as a seven-metre cyclonic swell surged in, shattering a shipwreck below.

Demelza now lives in Perth, Western Australia, the shark attack capital of the world.

The *Ocean's Gift* series was her first foray into fiction, followed by her suspense thriller *Nightmares* trilogy. She swears the *Mel Goes to Hell* series ambushed her on a crowded train and wouldn't leave her alone.

Want to know more? You can follow Demelza on Facebook, Twitter, YouTube or her website, Demelza Carlton's Place at:

www.demelzacarlton.com

More Books by Demelza Carlton

<u>Colony: Holiday series</u>

Cowboys and Aliens (#1)

Ghost (#2)

Vulcan (#3)

Cupid (#4)

Valentine(#5)

Prometheus (#6)

<u>**Colony: Aqua series**</u>

Halcyon (#1)

Poseidon (#2)

Apollo (#3)

<u>**Siren of War series**</u>

Ocean's Justice (#1)

Ocean's Widow (#2)

Ocean's Bride (#3)

Ocean's Rise (#4)

Ocean's War (#5)

How To Catch Crabs

<u>**Nightmares Trilogy**</u>

Nightmares of Caitlin Lockyer (#1)

Necessary Evil of Nathan Miller (#2)

Afterlife of Alana Miller (#3)

Romance a Medieval Fairytale series

Enchant: Beauty and the Beast Retold

Dance: Cinderella Retold

Fly: Goose Girl Retold

Revel: Twelve Dancing Princesses Retold

Silence: Little Mermaid Retold

Awaken: Sleeping Beauty Retold

Embellish: Brave Little Tailor Retold

Appease: Princess and the Pea Retold

Blow: Three Little Pigs Retold

Return: Hansel and Gretel Retold

Wish: Aladdin Retold

Melt: Snow Queen Retold

Spin: Rumpelstiltskin Retold

Kiss: Frog Prince Retold

Reflect: Snow White Retold

Roar: Goldilocks Retold

Cobble: Elves and the Shoemaker Retold

Float: Enchanted Horse Retold

Steal: Forty Thieves Retold

Call: Pied Piper Retold

Fall: Scheherazade Retold

Feather: Swan Maidens Retold

Curse: Rose Red Retold

Cross: Billy Goats Gruff Retold

Weave: Rapunzel Retold

Claim: Puss in Boots Retold